Publisher's Note: This is a work of fiction. Names, characters, places, and incidents are a product of the author's imagination. Locales and public names are sometimes used for atmospheric purposes. Any resemblance to actual people, living or dead, or to businesses, companies, events, institutions, or locales is coincidental.

Edited by Aquila Editing

Cover Designer: Cormar Covers

❋ Created with Vellum

DECKED

ABBY KNOX

Summary

Ally

What could be more lucky than having a successful brother who includes you on his luxury charter-yacht vacation in the Mediterranean? Sun, sea breeze, cute deckhands, and beach reads seems like the perfect getaway from my aimless life. Except for one thing: the tacit understanding here is that I'll be working for my brother's gaming company. No thanks! I'm only 19 once, and when am I ever coming back to Italy? I intend to make the most of it while I'm here, even if the captain insists that my flighty ass needs a grumpy, tattooed deckhand to chaperone me on a shopping excursion. This guy had better batten down the hatches, because we're about to have some fun with my trust fund.

Quint

I didn't sign up to work on the deck of The Carpe Diem only to spend time following a 19-year-old rich kid around Naples. But I need to stop punching coworkers in the face if I don't want to end up on babysitting duty.

However, spending the day with Ally soon proves to be more than what anyone bargained for. Figuring out that she's perfect for me doesn't take long. There's just one problem: she's a guest, and I'm not allowed to touch her. Not in the way I want to. I'll have to wait until her charter is over. Waiting…that's the wisest course of action for two impulsive people, right?

Naughty Yachties is a new series of short romance stories loosely inspired by Below Deck. If you love romance tropes, obsessed heroes, plucky heroines, high heat, and happily ever afters, then welcome aboard!

Chapter One

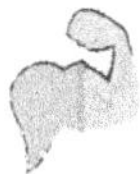

Ally

A SHADOW SLIDES across the page of this book I'm intently
reading, and now, all the words are illegible.

Assuming this is a cloud problem, I don't look up.
Instead, I squint at the page. I need to finish this chapter.

And yet, I sense something else. Someone is watching
me. That someone smells like wood polish, glass cleaner,
and not unpleasant sweat. It's a man, isn't it? A man is
staring at me, pulling me right out of my book.

There must be some law of nature that states that no
matter where I sit down to read, someone must show up to
stand in my light. Even at the tippy-top level of this behe-
moth yacht on the sunniest day that the Mediterranean has
ever seen, probably.

"You make a better door than a window," I say,
glancing up.

I can't identify the owner of the silhouette, other than

it belongs to a lean, masculine frame. He's got to be one of the deckhands I met when I boarded this boat yesterday.

"Ma'am?"

The way he says it, I instantly know which one. The pale, dark-haired, American one. Quint. Unlike the Bahamian bosun named Elijah and the Brazilian guy named Andre, this one has tattoos and doesn't smile much. The rest of *The Carpe Diem* crew have been all smiles— almost too interested in my needs and comfort. This is why I ended up reading high atop the vessel, in what they call the "bunny pad," named, I guess, because it's the usual spot you're likely to find supermodels on a craft such as this? I don't know.

I slide my bookmark into place and close my novel. I lean back against the cushions and prop myself up on my elbows.

"I said, 'you make a better door than a window.' You're standing in my light."

He shifts to the right, and I raise my book to block the sun so I can take in his face. Rather than his eyes, my gaze lands on his chest, noticing how that polo shirt doesn't suit him very well. He would look better in a button-up shirt, like the dress whites he wore yesterday or the dress blacks from last night. Or…nothing.

God, Ally. Lonely much?

Noticing the sun beating down into my eyes, he shifts back to block the light. "Is there anything I can get you?"

I am a little thrown off by this question. I guess it's all business with this one and no friendly banter. "Uh, a flashlight if you're going to continue to stand there while I'm reading my book."

The man simply nods. "Juno asked me to see if you need anything."

Sarcasm isn't for everyone, I guess. At least he's cute. In a taciturn, unreadable sort of way.

The sun is getting pretty hot up here, so I suggest, "Sunscreen?"

"Yes, ma'am," he says crisply, handing out a small plastic bottle he happens to have on him.

I don't know if chatting up Quint is a good or bad idea, but I'm now wholly unable to focus on this book. I'm bored. I'm enjoying the challenge of breaking his perfect stuffed-shirt demeanor. And also, his scent is slowly becoming more and more attractive the longer he stands there.

Turning my back and looking up at him over my shoulder, I ask, "Rub some on my back for me?"

Quint freezes so abruptly that the air around us seems to still. He's holding the bottle out to me like he wants me to just take it and apply the sunscreen myself.

"Just the one spot right between my shoulder blades. Not even yoga can make me that flexible. I wouldn't ask if I didn't need help," I tell him.

"Sure. Let me radio Juno to help you with…." He trails off. I scramble to my feet. The ocean breeze from up here cools me in all the places I hadn't noticed were sweating through my beach blanket, and my core temperature lowers a bit.

"Nah," I reply. "No need. I think I'm in very capable hands."

I shouldn't mess with him. But I just…don't want him to leave. And why is that? My time would be better spent getting on with reading my book. I can't explain myself other than I haven't felt another human's hands on me in far too long.

Because Quint is a decent guy, he rubs the stuff

between his hands before applying it to my skin. "Appreciate it so much," I say.

He grimaces in response, approaching me with the white stuff on his hands, looking like I've asked him to dissect roadkill.

Two swipes, and he's done. "There you go," he says.

Now, I know the rules about touching guests. Fraternizing is a huge no-no. But come on. It may be a while before anyone touches me again, so I'll take the contact wherever I can.

"I'm so sorry, but could you rub it in for me?"

Quint's face goes from grimace to annoyance. Yikes. I guess I made it weird.

However, I'm pleasantly surprised that he does the job right this time. After another moment of hesitancy, his hands spread the substance slowly, working it into my skin. Rough fingers send sparks of heat through me that have nothing to do with the hot sun.

I do not know how long he takes because his caress is hypnotizing. I close my eyes and notice how my body reacts. Goosebumps spread across my neck. I feel pleasantly lightheaded.

This is the sort of feeling that occurs when my mind and body anticipation being kissed. I know that's not about to happen, but I give in to the momentary fantasy.

Quint finishes with an unintelligible noise of exertion that only men seem to make during hard work, originating somewhere deep in his body cavity. Geez. Did I ask him to build a house or apply sunscreen?

"There. You're covered," he mumbles.

I turn and smile, blinking up at him. "Thank you so much."

Even with his sunglasses on, I can tell he's not meeting my eyes but glancing out at the water, at the floor, anywhere but at me. "Gotta protect the skin," he says flatly.

Wow. Is this him trying to make conversation?

"Yes. The sun is hotter here than I'm accustomed to. I suppose you get used to it while working on boats. Do you enjoy it? It seems fascinating to me."

Quint's gaze skims to me, shifting his weight from one foot to the other. Conveniently, he touches his earpiece.

"Yes, Captain. On my way."

Guess that's a no on whether he's actually up for a chat about life on a boat. That wasn't small talk; I'm aimless, and a job on a yacht seems interesting. Way more interesting than "working" for my brother, the primary guest on this vessel.

Without so much as a nod in my direction, Quint turns to leave.

I can spot a fake phone call—or a fake radio call—from a mile away. And that was fake as fuck.

I can't blame him for making up an excuse to get away from a demanding guest. Is that what I am? I hadn't thought so. But I couldn't even get a smile out of that guy.

He must really hate my guts.

Chapter Two

Quint

THE CHIEF STEWARD, Juno, catches me on the way to my post. "There you are? Does Ally need anything?"

I pick up my squeegee and grunt. "No." This is where I preferred to be in the first place, where I'd been happily cleaning windows before my entire world was turned upside down.

It's not true, though. Ally needs something. Attention, and lots of it. Just not from me. Me? I need to stay far, far away.

Juno nods but then continues to stand there. I see her out of the corner of my eye, watching me clean the boat's windows. "Are you okay?"

"Yes," I say, but don't ask why she's asking.

"Huh. You seem pissed at me," she says.

Juno never backs down from a possible confrontation, so I scramble to think of something innocuous that won't bring up further questions. "I'm fine. I'm just behind now."

"Sorry about that. Maybe Elijah can speak to the captain about hiring another deckhand if me grabbing you for service for five minutes is setting you that far behind."

Guess I picked the wrong answer.

"I'm good," I say, squeegeeing even more vigorously. She notices how hard I'm pushing. I accidentally slop some water from the bucket onto the deck, splattering a little onto her feet.

"Sorry," I bite out.

She mutters before walking away, "Try not to break the windows, psycho."

I'll try. My whole body is wound so tight I might break anything I touch. Right is wrong. Wrong is right. And I am a creep whose cock has gone stiff over a filthy-rich 19-year-old. I focus on cleaning windows, swabbing the teak, whatever it takes to not have to think about Ally.

"Hey, Mister Personality. Next time I'll be happy to handle massaging the guests."

Fucking Dustin. Even as a third engineer now, he can't stop spying on everyone via the security monitors. He's gross.

He can say what he wants about me, but hearing him casually mention Ally's name raises my hackles.

Without turning around to face him, I answer, maybe a little too forcefully, "You won't be handling anyone but yourself, friend."

Because he just loves to poke the bear, he continues talking to me. "Hey, calm down. What's the matter? You got a crush on the primary's bratty little sister?"

I would like him to shut up and go away now. I will not be getting into a fight with him today. He's a third engineer, not even close to my rank on this boat. He's a shit-stirrer who resents getting reassigned because he can't stop tattling on every tiny perceived sin. He's not worth it.

"No, but that doesn't mean I want any of the guests having to suffer a troglodyte."

"Big word for a jarhead."

"That's the marines, idiot."

"Navy, Marines. How can I tell the difference? You're all short-tempered assholes who can't take a joke."

I do not care what this guy thinks. I really don't.

Just then, the third stew rushes past, seemingly in tears.

"Whoa, honey. Not so fast," Dustin says, reaching out to hook her arm as she passes. "What happened?"

Star pulls away from his touch and runs into the empty main salon. The second stew, Julia, is there, and they sit down to assess whatever just happened.

"I should go comfort her," Dustin says in a voice that is anything but sincere.

"I think you should let the interior handle whatever is going on and mind your own business."

"Hey, you can't claim every hot female ass on this boat for yourself. Wouldn't be fair."

My neck muscles tighten. I don't want him near anyone, let alone the women on this boat. Star, the youngest and the greenest of the crew, hasn't had the most outstanding track record for keeping up the pace this charter season, but she tries hard. The primary has already tried to get her fired for a poorly made margarita. Likely that's what has happened again.

"You're right, though," Dustin muses. "The third stew is more your speed, intellectually speaking."

Why does he keep pressing me? What is he up to?

Keep your head cool, Quint. "Running your mouth is what got you demoted, mate. Watch it."

Dustin takes a step toward me as I continue to work, and I can tell he's trying to intimidate me out of the corner of my eye. Trying to provoke me.

"I'm gonna show that brat upstairs how a real man uses his hands. Maybe you should watch and take notes, and you'll have better luck with the ladies."

One move is all it takes for me to put this kid on the floor before I reel my temper back in.

Dustin clutches his nose where I knocked him right in the schnozz with the hardest part of my arm, just above my elbow. That's what he gets for running his mouth while standing behind me. I didn't even have to aim, and I was already coiled and ready. Granted, I didn't do it hard enough to make him bleed. I wanted to, but I wouldn't want the stews to have more cleaning work on their hands.

I offer him help standing up, but he waves me away, still grunting in surprise and disgust at what I've done. He scurries off like a little bitch. I'll probably be in trouble for this one, but it will be worth it.

Sure enough. Moments later, I'm called up to the bridge with Elijah, the captain, and the first mate.

"No, I'm not sorry," I say to the captain. Elijah, my bosun, grimaces. "He was talking shit about the crew, specifically the women. And talking about propositioning the guests. Well, one guest in particular. The guy's an asshole."

Captain Joe grunts. He and Elijah share a knowing look, and I cross my arms in front of my chest.

The first mate shrugs. "As far as I'm concerned, this discipline meeting is a matter for your department, Elijah. I'll talk to Dustin on my end."

The captain dismisses the first mate, which leaves me with the other two who will decide my fate.

"If you're gonna fire me, fire me," I say to the captain.

Captain Joe sips his coffee and curses. "What is this, roofing tar?"

Elijah winces. "Star still hasn't caught on to the ratio of grounds to ounces in a pot."

The captain's face softens at the mention of Star. "Well, to be fair, it's fucked up math. The numbers on coffee pots don't mean anything by any system of measurements on this planet. I've always thought it was a conspiracy to make people run out of coffee faster."

Elijah and I exchange looks but say nothing about Captain Joe's brief but slightly unhinged rant about coffee ground ratios. Star is a sweet girl, but she is damn lucky this captain seems to have such a soft spot for her. He will jump through fiery hoops to give her chance after chance, proclaiming again and again that it's all about her good attitude.

The captain sets down his cup, claps his hands, and rubs his palms together. "Welp," he says. "Our top priority is always safety, followed by tending to the guests' wants. So that gives me an idea."

"I'm not fired?" I ask.

Captain Joe laughs. "Hell no. If I fired every deckhand that threw a punch at a fellow crew member, I'd have to start hiring robots. As efficient as they might be, robots don't seem that fun. So, back to my idea. The primary's sister, Ally, has requested a day trip onshore in Naples tomorrow. We usually send at least one crew member to chaperone guests when they take these excursions. Since this trip is just one guest, I'm assigning you to the job."

The captain gestures at me with his forehead. My brain short-circuits. No. No, this is a bad idea. "Me? And that teenager?"

The captain corrects me, "She's an adult, and she's a guest. Since you've shown an aptitude for protecting her, it only makes sense that you go."

I look at Elijah, who's nodding and rubbing his chin thoughtfully.

"What about the stews? I'm sure one of them would love to get outside for the day," I offer instead.

"The girls are busy with the primary and his gamer friends. Tomorrow they're starting their new…campaign, or whatever it's called, at eight a.m., and they aren't going to be leaving that sky deck to do much of anything for the next couple of days. I don't know why you'd need to bring your game company employees to one of the most beautiful spots in the world to just roll dice and talk about dragons. But here we are. The girls will be hopping, between bringing them snacks and drinks. That means you guys won't be needing to supervise any water sports."

Elijah says, "Which means you'll have some time on your hands."

I can't believe this is happening. But what can I do? I can't say no to Elijah. And I don't dare say no to the captain.

"Guess I'm chaperoning the kid tomorrow," I say, blowing out a breath.

As I stalk back to my bunk, I have to remind myself that this is a far better fate than getting fired.

Look at it this way, I tell myself. You got to punch Dustin in the face, and you were invited to put your hands on a girl's back. And not just any girl. Some type of goddess who left you thunderstruck before even making eye contact. All in all, pretty decent day.

Tomorrow, though? Tomorrow is going to be way too much of a good thing. So much that I'll be walking around Naples with a tent pole in my boxer briefs.

As I pick up my squeegee on the bow and get back to work cleaning the windows, I think about how to control myself around her all day. Cleaning and taking care of this boat is so much more straightforward. I don't ever have to worry about a random stiffy while doing my job.

So yeah, tomorrow? It's going to suck.

Chapter Three

Ally

My brother Denny is the only other guest awake for breakfast early the next day. Watching me as he hovers over a plate of eggs and pancakes, he looks more parental than like the role-playing-game mogul he is.

"I'd be more comfortable if you'd stick around today and get to know the team," he says, pouring maple syrup on his plate.

The thought of working for him at his gaming company makes me want to commit crimes. Crimes far worse than the ones I committed at 15, which he and the rest of the family can't seem to shake.

"I'm not going to shoplift if that's what you're worried about," I say, plopping down in one of the cozy sky deck dining chairs and plucking up a slice of bacon. Munching on it thoughtfully, I try to think of how to gracefully tell him I don't want anything to do with this nerdfest.

He bristles. It's as if saying the word "shoplift" out loud

embarrasses him. I did what I did; I worked it off. He's the only one who hasn't moved on.

Denny slices his pancakes, not making eye contact. "But why not take an opportunity to get to know the personalities you'll be working with? If I were you, I'd consider this an opportunity to learn the ropes of the company in a fun, no-pressure setting."

I smile at his wording and reply, "Did you know that show you the ropes' phrase comes from boat rigging?"

He says, "Yeah, obviously," I can tell he didn't know that. He also sounds a lot more like my brother than the parental tone he's been taking with me since I turned 18, graduated high school, and decided not to go to college.

I mimic his tone and mime pushing up glasses on the bridge of my nose. "Obviously."

Denny snorts and shakes his head, "Child." He then shoves so much food into his mouth that I can't believe the irony. He looks like he did at 14, eating like a lunatic to gross me out. I nibble on more bacon, then finally say, "Maybe I should learn how to work on a yacht? That seems fun."

He looks at me pointedly, pausing over his food. "Your own brother owns a gaming company. That is the definition of fun."

I narrow my eyes at him. "Sure. Shopping and vacation are more fun, so that's what I'm doing today."

Some of his employees start to arrive and find spots at the breakfast table. We exchange pleasantries, but Denny's parental face is back.

As I stand to leave, he points at me with the tines of his fork. "Just remember our budget agreement."

My stomach twists. He didn't have to remind me. I hate that I don't have a job yet and don't know what I want to do.

We have agreed to let him control my trust fund and give me allowances for my needs and wants until I start a career. I don't love that, but I understand it. Still, why would he feel the need to humiliate me like that in front of his employees?

I stalk away wordlessly, mentally fighting off the dark cloud that my brother has just cast over what was supposed to be a lovely day out by myself.

When the tattooed one greets me in the tender, ready to cast off the yacht and motor to shore, I speak before I think. "They couldn't have sent one of the stews with me instead?"

This was the wrong question to ask Quint, who, for a second, looks a little bit flustered as he helps me hop into the small motorboat that accompanies *The Carpe Diem.*

"I got in trouble, so this is my punishment," he says.

I could be offended, but instead, I laugh, assuming he's joking. "Well, it's an apt consequence for whatever you did because this will probably not be any fun."

He doesn't reply, only starts the engine.

Neither of us says much for the first hour or so of the morning onshore, and I'm grateful for the crowded streets in the touristy area of the city. The noise of other people having fun overpowers the need to try to make small talk—and clearly, this guy hates small talk.

I wind my way through the street stalls, occasionally stopping to look at jewelry, sunglasses, sandals, and trinkets. I look back at Quint. I may as well be invisible. Some chaperone.

Quint unexpectedly moves in close to me when I purchase some small souvenirs. I suck in a breath as I'm overwhelmed by his…everything. That tattoo on his neck is in my face, the heat of his body radiates off of him, and his scent…oh my gosh, he smells even better than yesterday. Still of cleaning products but also something else. Did he put on cologne?

I don't know what I thought he was about to do to me, but I thought wrong. He snatches the bag out of my hand.

"You don't have to carry my things."

He says abruptly, "It's safer if strangers assume we are…together."

I'm laughing on the outside, but on the inside, I melt. Taking a deep breath to calm my nerves at his continued closeness, I say, "I like that game. Let's pretend we're a couple."

"That's not at all what I—"

I reach up and touch the tip of his nose with the end of my index finger. "Teasing. But come on, it's fun to get off the boat, isn't it?"

Quint is silent, then asks, "Did you just boop my nose?"

I've seen this man talking and joking with his fellow crewmates. So, I know he has the capacity for fun. To carry on a conversation and not look utterly miserable while doing his job.

"Yes?" I answer, not totally sure of anything anymore. I've always thought I was a fun person to be around, but maybe not.

While we're standing here face to face, I look into those dark eyes and try to figure out what he could be thinking. Does he hate me? Hate his job? Hate Italy?

"Please, do not touch me," he says.

I slowly suck in a breath. His jaw ticks. "I'm sorry," I say, putting my hand back on the bag of my souvenirs. "But you don't have to carry my things for me. This is not a high school romance drama."

At the word *romance*, Quint's eyes flash at mine. "I don't

have any plans to be involved with you if that's what you mean."

Taking a step back, I survey his body language and finally understand. It's me. "Wow, okay, calm down, Quint. I know you find me revolting, but I was kidding about the romance part."

His eyes narrow, saying, "Who told you I found you revolting?"

I raise both eyebrows. "You didn't need to say the exact words, but I felt it when you slapped sunscreen on me and sprinted away."

"Did I misapply it?" Quint blinks at me, a face of total confusion.

Improperly? The man's hands sent ripples of need down my spine. My body was still humming from that contact when I went to sleep last night. "In the end, yeah. But you acted like I had violated you by asking in the first place."

The look of chagrin on his face. I can't take it. What is the message you're trying to send, boy?

"Listen, it's fine. You don't have to pretend. It's not like I'm a supermodel, or an influencer, like some of the other guests you're used to. I know I'm not a size zero and six foot two."

Quint once again looks lost for words. But then steps toward me, so close that I feel compelled to take a step backward, right into a display of earrings.

I didn't think he was that big and tall, but he has a way of taking up space, towering over me, and making me feel like he's everywhere. "You're not a supermodel. Your body is fine. Perfect, actually. Perfectly nice, and your skin is… very nice. I don't care about size. I tried to be professional and not let you think I was crossing any lines. I was in a hurry because I don't know if technically I'm allowed to apply sunscreen."

Am I an idiot, or is he just really good at poker? One minute I can read him like a book, and the next minute I have no idea what's happening. "So you don't hate me?"

"I've never hated anyone. Least of all you."

We hold this moment for I don't know how long.

"What…exactly is happening right now?" I ask.

Suddenly, as if he has snapped himself out of a trance, he steps back. "That," he says, with a look in his eyes so heated it could melt ice from across the street, "was some lines getting blurred. I warn you, don't tempt me to break the rules ever again."

I wonder if this man is too intense for a shopping day with little ol' me. I don't know how much more I can stand it if every interaction turns into a whole thing.

"Fine," I say, crossing my arms. "Just keep your distance, then. I'm going shopping. You do you, babe. Enjoy your day. If you can keep up."

I whirl away and speed-walk up the street, weaving through more vendors selling jewelry, scarves, works of art. I pick up a few more items here and there.

"Seriously. I got it," I tell Quint when he's on top of me again, taking my bag.

"Not an option," he tells me.

"It's not your job to carry all my shit. You're just supposed to chaperone me."

He says nothing but continues to stalk behind me everywhere I go.

I take advantage of a passing crowd of tourists to duck into a shoe store without him. He's been breathing down my neck, and I'd rather shop with someone who likes me. And so far, the only person who likes me on this trip is me.

Chapter Four

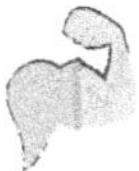

Quint

A GROUP of tourists blocks my view just as I see Ally crossing the street. I weave around them, and she's gone.

I don't see her anywhere.

Is this how my career ends? I lose the primary's little sister?

Well, shit.

With my hands on my hips, I scan the crowds, the stores, the vendors. Where would I go if I were a 19-year-old girl? I mean, woman. Shit.

That shoe store? It looks like the kind of place she might like. Bright colors, designer monstrosities in the window. I duck inside and immediately feel out of place.

But I don't care about that feeling. She's here.

It occurs to me that the anxiety over losing her is quickly becoming less about my job and more about something else. What is it? What am I feeling? All the lines I've drawn are starting to blur, and I have to close my eyes and put them back into place.

I'm not making any sense. I just have to do my job, get this day over with, and go back to the boat, where the two of us can be supervised by literally dozens of pairs of eyes. One thing is for sure, I'm the one that needs a chaperone. Not Ally.

Another emotion takes hold of me when I see her chatting with a salesman over a pair of designer heels that look more like art than practical shoes. Where exactly is she going to wear those?

And then, I see what's happening. The man who kneels in front of her is stroking her feet. Her adorable little feet and stubby toes. I watch in horror as he runs a finger along the bottom of her arch, talking some bullshit about her high arches and foot width and whatnot.

"Hey, I'm ticklish," she squeals. The man stops his itchy fingers and bows his head in apology, but he still doesn't move his hands away from her feet.

I watch his fingers smooth over the inside of her ankle as he continues talking some horse shit about her feet. To make matters worse, he speaks in a thick Italian accent that I know Ally must be swooning over. I can't handle it. Something comes over me. I don't know if I am overreacting, but suddenly, I want to grab her and march her out of here.

I'm going to lose it. I'm going to embarrass the boat. But at this moment, watching another man touch her, I'm past the point of caring about that.

<h1 style="text-align:center">Chapter Five</h1>

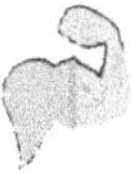

Ally

"Let's go."

A man's gruff voice is accompanied by rough hands tugging me to my feet.

"Quint! I am trying on shoes!" I can feel my cheeks burning in embarrassment as the salesman has reared back in self-defense.

"Not from this guy." Quint's nostrils are flared like he's pissed, like I've done something wrong.

"Yes, I am!" I insist.

"Put your sandals on; we're leaving."

I try to jerk my hand away from him, but not really. "But Daddy," I say, jutting out my bottom lip. "You said I could have anything I wanted for my birthday."

The salesman says something I don't understand in Italian. There's a flash of something dark across Quint's face. He takes a beat. And then I see something like a hint of a smile pulling at his lip before he trains his face.

"Little girl," Quint rasps. "I told you what would happen the next time I caught you flirting with another man. Do you need a spanking to remind you?"

He's playing along. He's actually playing along! I knew Quint could be fun. It takes every ounce of self-control for me not to break character right now. I started it, and somehow we are going to finish this scene. I look from Quint to the salesman and back to Quint, my mouth turned down in a fake frown, phony tears welling up in my eyes.

"I'm sorry, Daddy. I didn't mean to." I gesture around wildly. "Everyone is so sweet to me, and I'm a nice person. Sometimes it's hard for me to tell when someone is flirting."

I step forward, and Quint shoots me a warning glance, brows raised. He's trying to say, don't move an inch. But I take another step. His eyes widen. He knows only that he has no idea what I will do next.

"Just don't let it happen again," he grumbles.

My hand palms his forearm, and I run my fingers upward, along the sinews, the tight muscle, and over his bicep. Oh lord, I was not prepared for how much I might enjoy touching his body. Keep it together, Ally. I look up at him, and my roaming hand automatically goes to his chest, his sternum, where a racing heart beats under all that hardness. My face would go nicely here, right here on his chest. This is where I would fit next to him if we were to… if he were to snuggle me after sex. Being this close to him and sensing how well we might click together, move together, get lost together — I almost forget that every pair of eyes in the shoe store is on us.

Gathering my senses, I gaze up at him sheepishly. "But…" I start, biting my lip for extra drama. "Can I still have the shoes? For my birthday? Daddy?" I over-enunciate the last two Ds like a silly little girl. Right on cue, Quint's jaw ticks. I can no longer tell if he's acting or truly pissed at me. Coming up on my toes, I murmur loud enough for someone nearby to hear us. "I'll wear them while you do that thing you love."

Quint lets out a long, noisy breath like trying to cleanse himself of demons.

He stalks to the register without releasing my hand and plonks down his card. Wow. When he commits to a skit, he really commits. I am impressed. I never would have thought he had it in him.

Outside on the street, he finally lets go of my hand.

"Well, that was fun!" I laugh, feeling light, alive, and giddy.

Quint, however, runs both his hands over his face and through his hair and won't look at me.

"Hey," I say, gesturing up the hill. "I see a bank up there. I'll get a cash advance on the card and pay you back for the shoes."

His hands come away from his face, and he looks at me. Just stares. Then his eyes fall to my feet, and again his hands rub over his chin, his fingers digging into his stubble along his jaw.

"Keep your money."

"Quint!"

He walks away, and I follow. Funny, he's supposed to be the one following me around.

That was a $400 pair of shoes!" I remind him.

"And?"

"And I'm pretty sure that violates some kind of rule of the boat."

"Not that I know of."

I am unsure of what to say next. So I stop chasing and just watch him.

"You didn't just pay for my shoes for the bit, Quint?"

He bites out, "I had to get you out of there. That guy had his hands all over your feet."

I lift my knee and show him the magnificent heels I now wear. "He was measuring me!"

"For what?"

"Shoes, Quint! Shoes!"

"I didn't see one of those metal things with numbers anywhere, did you?"

The way the cords in his neck stand out when he hisses at me is adorable. Threatening but adorable. I would nibble on them if he'd let me. I point back at the shoe store. "He doesn't need one of those thingies! He's an expert."

The derisive noise that comes out of Quint scares away a couple of pigeons who have been sharing a crust of bread on the street. "I'm surprised at how naïve you are about how he was so obviously coming on to you. I can't allow strange men to be touching you like that when I'm responsible for you."

Naive is the wrong word to say to me. I explode, completely untethered from reality. "Maybe if everyone climbed down off my ass for one second instead of assuming I need supervision like a delinquent adolescent, I would be less naïve!"

As soon as the outburst is out of my mouth, I regret it. I regret being so loud and angry, and most of all, I regret projecting my problems onto a man who has no idea what my life is like.

He looks utterly confused, and I feel embarrassed. I don't want to explain these feelings that brought that on. So, I do what I do best. I turn tail and run.

Chapter Six

Quint

Fᴜᴄᴋ ᴍᴇ, she ditched me again.

It's now 11 a.m., and the crowds are starting to pick up, further hampering my ability to stay on top of Ally. A part of me is worried because I will indeed be fired if I lose her. I also know she's too ripe for the picking in this city. She's too beautiful, young, and innocent to be here on her own. I should not have said she was naïve, but the fact remains, she trusts people too easily.

I don't know what else to do, so I dart into one store after another, up and down the central shopping district. Eventually, I'm so distraught my mind plays tricks on me. Should I stay in one place and let her find me instead? But after our little exchange, I don't think she'll make an effort to find me and will, in fact, most likely put as much distance between us as possible.

I hit three more shoe stores, five dress stores, a couple

of coffee shops, and a handful of restaurants and bakeries, and nothing.

One more. One more, and I'm calling Elijah for reinforcement. If she's not in this dress shop, maybe we can get her phone number from the provisioning sheets without alerting her brother that we can't find her. Why I left the boat without her phone number is beyond me. Now, I doubt she would give it to me in the first place.

As I enter this shop, all I see at first is a sea of black and white street clothes and party dresses. But then, at the back of the store, I see long black tresses whip around the corner. I stalk to the back of the shop, ignoring the friendly greetings of the salespeople, and eat up the distance between Ally and me.

Around the corner, a diminutive saleswoman stops me in my tracks. "Pardon me. No."

"It's okay. He's just the bodyguard my brother hired to make sure I don't shoplift," I hear Ally say as she slips into one of the stalls in the row of dressing rooms.

Shoplift? I think I missed something in the brief for this assignment.

"I am not your bodyguard. I am your chaperone. There is a difference."

"Potato, potahto. Listen, I'm shopping for a dress… for dinner with the captain tonight. I'll try not to steal it if you can believe it."

I'm not supposed to let her out of my sight. And if she's going to try to push my buttons, run away every other minute, then she can't be trusted to be alone. So, going against every gentlemanly instinct, I let myself into her dressing room.

"Are you for real? Get out," Ally huffs.

"No, ma'am. I'm not letting you out of my sight again. Not after you ran away from me twice."

"What do you think I'm going to do from here? Shimmy through the air vent?" She performs a slight shake of her hips while peeling off her shirt. Holy hell. Swiftly, I turn around and face the wall of the dressing room.

"To get away from a pain in the ass like me? I suppose you'd try anything."

"You're not wrong."

Outside, the saleswoman tells us in Italian that she does not allow any funny business in dressing rooms. Still, I hear her footfalls disappear around the corner.

Turning my attention back to Ally, I ask her, over my shoulder, "What did I do that made you run away? I need to know because I can't keep up with whatever narrative is going on in your head."

Fabric moves and shifts, and out of the corner of my eye, I see her skin is covered again, and I turn around. Ally's back is to me, where a polka dot dress hangs open at the back zipper. Her bare shoulders are sun-kissed, and I notice the pattern of freckles dotting her skin. I look past her shoulder into the mirror, where she's holding up the dress's bodice, her hands cupping the fabric under her breasts. Her eyes stare back at me in a question. Over her shoulder, she gestures with her chin. "Since you're here, could you zip me up, please?"

Again, she wants me to put my hands on her? After the way she spoke to me in the street? After the way I nearly yanked her out of the shoe store? What's going on with her?

"Are you sure you don't want to ask the sales lady?"

The mirror reflects her lip curling up with a subtle smirk. "Why, so you can lose your damn mind the second time a professional puts their hands on me?"

She's not wrong. "I take my job seriously."

My thick fingers fumble with the delicate metal zipper,

and I know I'm going to get it caught in the fabric and ruin this…whatever this is. Silk? Chiffon? I have no fucking idea. And yet, the zipper slides up smoothly, and the dress hugs her curves perfectly as if it were made for her.

Ally's face cracks into a wide smile at herself. She looks incredible, of course.

"What do you think?"

This is a dangerous question. But I tell her what I really think. "I don't know about clothes and things, but this dress looks like something you would wear to brunch and not a formal dinner. Also, I think the pattern is too matronly for you."

"Really? Huh. I never would have thought that" she says, spinning around and examining her ass and hips in the mirror. "You know what? You're right. Let me try the white dress."

I move to turn around to once again face the wall, and she scoffs. "Friend, my undies cover a hell of a lot more than my bikini, so you might as well stay put."

"Oh, I don't think that's a good idea. Oh my god."

Sometimes her selective hearing comes at the most opportune moments. Still, I am frozen to the spot while watching her tanned body wiggle and jiggle out of the polka dot dress and hand it to me. My hands sweat all over the fabric while I slip it back onto the hanger and hook it on the outside of the door.

When I turn around, I am not prepared to see Ally in white lace. The sight of her splits me open like a burst of lightning. She looks…bridal and sexy. The dress falls just below her tush, and the back is nonexistent, calling to mind all sorts of inappropriate thoughts that make my dick twitch. There are only about six inches of zipper between her cheeks. Holy shit. If I look too closely, I can see the shadow of her split above her panties. If she were mine, I could take her from behind without even removing that dress. I would fucking own that ass. Get lost in it and never come out. I would die a happy man between those cheeks. I could slide my hands along the edges of that lace and handle those tits of hers. All that exposed skin of her back, I would cover with nibbles.

I force myself to breathe and zip her up.

Gazing at her in the mirror, I see something else. The front neckline sweeps across her delicate collarbones, with bits of lacy floral vines swagging across her upper arms. She looks like a slutty fairy princess bride. She looks like my slutty fairy princess bride. Our eyes meet in the mirror, and I can't hide the expression on my face.

"Well, what about this one?" Ally bites her bottom lip anxiously.

I can barely breathe. So many thoughts are swimming through my head, but the one I land on is utterly pointless. "Not much of a zipper."

"Too much? Not enough?"

It's then that I notice my hands. They rest on her hips, and I do not remember putting them there. And she's not pushing me away. Cursing my impropriety but closing in on her anyway, I reply, "I don't know why my opinion matters to you."

I'm so close behind her that some of her flyaway hairs graze my cheek. She smells like something faintly floral and spicy and costly.

When she replies, her words have an almost unnotice-able tremor. "You've seen how people dress for these dinners. I haven't. So, your opinion matters."

It could be wishful thinking, but she might have backed up half an inch.

She's 19, and she's a guest. She's 19, and she's a guest. I repeat this mantra, but it is starting to lose all meaning, replaced by the scent of her shampoo in my nose, the vision of my future wife in the mirror.

"Well, my opinion is if you wear this dress, you should wear your hair up so everyone can see the details."

Dangerous. This is really fucking dangerous right now.

A small pink tongue darts out to wet her lips, and I could be mistaken, but it feels as if her eyes are studying my mouth. "The details of the dress?" The question is breathy.

"No. I mean this." Letting go of her hips, I wrap both hands around the length of her hair and gently twist it up, revealing her neck.

Her eyes flutter closed, briefly, when I touch her like this. "I mean the details of…you."

Nostrils flaring, eyes wide, her cheeks turn pink. Once again, she chews on her bottom lip, and I have to fight the urge to spin her around to me and claim it as mine to nibble.

She breathes, "I yelled at you before because I thought we were having fun, but then what you said after that…it's not your fault, but I was reminded that I haven't grown up in anybody's eyes. When I was fifteen, I went through a brief shoplifting phase. I stole some clothes, some jewelry. A guy friend at the time saw how good I was at it and started using me to steal stuff for him to sell for money. It got out of hand, and I spent some time on house arrest, and he went to juvie. I had bodyguards, chaperones, whatever you want to call it, every second until I turned 18. I've never done anything really on my own. I'm still 15 in my parents' eyes. They and my brother decided this trip would be good for me. Denny walks on water and…I don't know; I guess they think I'll decide on a career by just being around him? I've barely had time to think for myself, let alone know what I want to do with my life. So that's my story."

I am frozen in place, still holding her hair, just listening.

Every word she said squeezes my heart. "I can see you're not that 15-year-old anymore," I rasp. "You're fun and interesting and funny. Maybe you need to like yourself a little bit more."

She smiles in the mirror, examining how I'm holding up her long locks in a twist.

"I…I like my shoulders," she says softly, rolling her shoulders back and…leaning? Yes, she's leaning back. Our bodies are touching. I'm so close I could lick her skin Without much effort. And her scent. Holy shit, I might be drunk on her.

"So do I," I blurt without thinking, my nose grazing over the expanse of her neck, her bare shoulders. Ally sucks in a breath and falls against me. At that moment, everything changes. She fits so perfectly against me. Every curve of her body nests against my every ridge and plane. My world is about to fall apart or come together; I can't tell which.

We lock eyes in the mirror, and for a brief second, it's just her and just me. One arm snakes around her waist, and her eyes flick down to watch. I hold her tight against me, knowing she can feel me, feel how hard I am, how the length of me reacts to being so close to her. A deeper red flushes her cheeks, and her lips part.

"You should like all of you. All of you is fucking delicious." I have no idea if what I said was grammatically correct. I don't care. I just need…I just need…

All it takes is one pass of my mouth against the side of her neck, and she jerks away from me.

"I'm sorry," I say.

Flustered, she turns to face me, hands wringing. "No, I'm sorry. I shouldn't have asked you to help me."

"Don't stress about it. It's my job to maintain a boundary, not yours."

Something crosses her face that I don't quite understand. "I always go off the rails. I'm just supposed to buy a dress and some accessories, then go back to the boat. But now I'm almost kissing a man twice my age who's supposed to be my chaperone."

I put up a hand. "Listen, I'm 27, not twice your age."

"Still," she says. "I shouldn't be flirting with you. It wouldn't be right."

I open my mouth to speak, but she stiffens. "Could you ask the sales lady to come to help me with the zipper? I'll meet you outside."

"You know that's not happening, right?"

She begs me. "Please, Quint. Just one minute of space to breathe. Please."

Everything on her face plucks at my heartstrings. How can I say no to that?

Moments pass as I wait on the bench outside the dress shop, waiting to carry her garment bags on top of her shoes and trinkets. I watch happy couples stroll by. I obligingly snap some photos of a few who want poses by the fountain.

All the while, my heart hammers against my ribs. In that mirror, I had seen my future. Ally may regret behaving like a temptress, but she didn't do anything wrong. What she doesn't know is she already belongs to me.

I sit there and mentally plan out our entire future. It doesn't occur to me until many minutes later that she's taking far too long in that store.

Popping my head inside, she's not there. In my terrible Italian, I ask the same woman who spoke to us earlier if she's seen the young woman. The owner looks at me like I'm nuts. In English, she tells me she left ten minutes ago.

I run back outside and realize that this girl has given me the slip once again.

And that's when I notice the bookstore.

Chapter Seven

Ally

MY BROTHER CALLS while I'm extremely busy drooling over the books in the English language section of this beautiful bookshop. My bagged dress hooked over my arms is already cumbersome, and now I have to answer the phone, too?

"Hi, Denny, what's up?"

I'm about to tell him about the fabulous dress I just bought for the big seven-course dinner with the captain tonight, but I can sense my brother is hot about something.

"Where are you, and what did you just pay for?"

Bewildered, I tell him, "I bought a dress; why?"

"I just got a notification for $700, and I thought it was a fraudulent charge. That was you?"

"I didn't check the price tag, but it's well under the total of what I've spent on clothes this month," I reply. "And From what I understand, tonight's dinner is formal attire. Look where we are; this is not Wal-Mart country."

"I never said you had a Wal-Mart budget, but I need you to understand this is not the way you manage your money."

Now, I'm starting to get a little heated myself. I remind him it's him managing my money, but he's not the one doing the actual shopping and wouldn't understand.

"You need to return the dress and get something more reasonable."

The beginning of angry tears stings my eyes. Once again, I have fucked up in my brother's eyes. But there's another reason I'm upset. The memory of how Quint looked at me in the mirror when I wore that dress. I felt when he looked at me like I was precious and perfect. Nobody ever looks at me like that. I can't bear it. The thought of returning that dress breaks my heart. It's just a piece of fabric, but maybe it's more than that.

"I just don't know when you'll trust me to be an adult. How much more do I have to pay for what I did." I hate that I can hear the wobble in my voice.

Denny sighs in a way that lets me know I'm a burden. "Listen, you're not in trouble. I set it up so I'd get a text regarding big purchases, so now you know that's too much, and you can correct yourself."

"Stop training me like a dog."

"That's not what this is."

"That's what it feels like."

Denny sighs in exasperation. "Consider this just a gentle check-in. Now exchange the dress and come back to the boat. You've had enough fun for one day."

"I am an adult."

"And later, we'll talk about how to spend money like an adult."

"Exactly," I say, seething. "So get the family attorney

on the phone because I want you out of my financial business."

"Come on, Ally."

I hang up, switch my phone to silent, and turn my attention to the book in my hand. It's the last book in the fantasy series that I'm reading, only in hardcover at the moment. Turning it over and checking the price, I know this — along with the rest of the stack that I'm drooling over —Will provoke another phone call from Denny. I could get a refund on the dress and buy these books, I suppose… But. But what? Why exactly don't I want to return the dress to the shop? That little moment in the dressing room … does it actually mean anything? If I keep the dress, won't it just be to throw it in my brother's face? And remind Quint of what he can't have? What I can't have?

What do I want more? The dress or the books?

Finally, I make my decision. The shopkeeper agrees to hold my stack of books until I return, and I promise to come back shortly.

With tears blurring my vision, I head back to the dress shop. Within minutes, I've returned the dress, much to the chagrin of the grumpy dress shop owner. In faltering Italian, I ask if she has anything on sale. Maybe I can split the difference and get both the books and the dress. But the way she stares me down, I decide it's better to simply ditch this idea and find a dress elsewhere.

Back out on the streets, I don't know what to do with myself. I feel sick to my stomach at returning that beautiful white dress. It makes no sense. Why do I care about that dress so much? Because I felt so beautiful in it? Because of Quint?

I can no longer deny it. Something about him gets to me. He's more than just the hot deckhand that awkwardly applied sunscreen on my back and got me all horny. Quint has sunk himself into my brain and into my bloodstream.

What the hell is happening To me? I never let a man get in the way of my reading. Suck it up, little girl.

I should just go back to the bookstore and buy the entire stack of books, head back to the boat and forget this day ever happened. Lose myself in some good stories.

Walking out of the dress shop with a heavy but determined heart, I slam into a brick wall of man.

"Quint!"

"Hi," he says.

"Hi," I say, biting my lip.

He smiles. "I wasn't going to chastise you for leaving me."

I look at his arms, both filled with bags. In one hand, he has two huge bags from the bookstore. "I didn't know you were a reader."

"I'm not. But these are not for me."

"Who are they for?"

People are milling around us, filling the tables of the outdoor cafes, and the aroma of delicious food makes my stomach roll in hunger.

"These are your books. The ones you left on the counter."

Wait, what? He didn't. There's no way.

I take a beat to study his face. There's a hint of something there behind his stoic exterior. He's proud of himself. I don't know whether to kick him or kiss him for interfering. Again.

I ask, swallowing hard, "How did you know?"

Quint smiles. It's a half smile, but it's a start. "Sweetheart, I can give you space, but I'm still going to keep my eye on you no matter how hard you try to get me fired."

This makes me laugh. Until I remember what he just

did. "You didn't have to do that. You shouldn't have done that. You paid for my shoes and now the books? I was coming back to get the books."

He shrugs. "I know."

"I returned the dress so I could have the books." Now, I'm feeling lightheaded, and I need to sit. I perch myself on the edge of the fountain and figure out what I'm feeling. I look down, and a pigeon cocks its little head at me. I scowl at it.

"You shouldn't have to choose," Quint says.

"I had to choose," I reply, unable to look at him. Into those intense dark eyes. Too much. He did too much.

"No, you didn't."

"Quint."

"Ally."

I smile but curse to myself. We sound like an old married couple having a fight. And him, with two bookstore shopping bags, a shoebox, and another bag full of my trinkets. He looks like a long-suffering husband on his wife's shopping trip.

Ultimately I'm unable to resist touching the books. Sorting through the bags, I run my hands over the hardcovers, admiring the lovely illustrations. It's all there, except one. I don't want to seem ungrateful, but the very book I wanted, the last one in the series I'm currently reading, isn't there. "Oh," I say, "I think you forgot one. I'll just head back inside and—"

"Here," Quint says, handing me the same book.

I look at him incredulously. "Why were you hiding that one behind your back?"

Gruffly, he replies. "No reason."

Cutting my eyes between him and the book, I slowly open the front cover and begin to flip through, smoothing my hands over the creamy pages. My hands freeze when I come to the title page. Something is scrawled there, and my instinct is to shout about people vandalizing books.

"What is this?" But when I take a closer look, I realize that it looks like the author's signature.

I drop the book on the bench and cover my mouth, shrieking. "Fuck me, what did you do?"

"I didn't do anything. The shopkeeper said they had some signed copies in stock, so I thought you'd appreciate that."

My entire body feels like it's floating, and I hate it. He's making me fall in love with him.

"Quint. This is amazing. This is too much. You are doing too much for me."

He makes a noise like an angry bull, huffing at an enemy. "Fuck that noise," he says.

I cannot tell if this sudden change in tone makes my blood run hot or cold.

"Excuse me?"

"I said, fuck that noise. Fuck Denny. Fuck anyone who made you think you don't deserve anything your heart desires."

My breathing goes shallow, and I ball my fists. "You buy me shoes, you buy me books, with some expectation… of what?"

Cursing under his breath, Quint tugs the book out of my hands and stuffs it back into the bag. Then, he cups my face and says, "Look at me. I bought you the books because I followed you through that store and watched you pick up every single one. I saw that you wanted them. I watched you read the backs, the first pages, run your hands over the paper, smile at the covers. You love this shit, so you should have it. That's all. I don't have any expectations based on that. I don't have any expectations at all. I'm simply telling you to tell everyone else who doesn't respect you or allow you to let go of your past to fuck right off."

He has to know what all of this looks like, even though my heart is telling me, screaming at me, that I've met a good one. That this might be the one. "I've led you on, and I'm sorry."

"Don't be sorry. You didn't lead me on."

"I didn't?"

There's nowhere to look while he's gripping my face like this, and his intensity is too much.

"You've been told this narrative. But that's not what I see. I see a good person who's still figuring out what she wants to do with her life. And that's fine. How could you believe that you led me on when I fell for you the second we met?"

I gasp. My heart races. "But the sunscreen…you were so grumpy about it. I swear you hated my guts."

He shrugs. "That's just the face I make when I'm horny. I love your guts."

Boiling. My blood is boiling. "Well, there's nothing we can do about that. We can't sleep together on the boat. We have no privacy."

He smiles wide now, and it's good that I'm sitting because my knees just went weak at seeing his teeth. Finally, he lets go of my face, and I breathe. "I spent eight years in the navy, and we had zero privacy, but we get it done," he says.

This makes me rage with jealousy and with horniness equally.

Sarcasm never far from my lips, I tell him, "If you're trying to get me to fall at your feet, stories about rushed hookups aboard an aircraft carrier is a sure-fire strategy, my guy."

That noise. What is it with him and these primal noises

every time he doesn't like my words? He lifts his chin at me and replies, "I ain't trying to get you to fall at my feet; I'm trying to get you to fall on my dick."

The absolute audacity of this man who was silent, awkward, and deeply uncomfortable around me only a few hours ago—I can't fathom what happened.

Several seconds pass while I try to think of a response to that.

"Then why haven't you kissed me yet, sailor?"

Quint's lips descend on mine far more gently than I would have expected from him. His personality that switches from stoic to grumpy to heated made me assume he would be eating my face at the first green light from me.

But no. Here he is, cupping my face in his hands, pressing our lips together in a long, sweet, soft kiss. He follows this by brushing his lips over mine in a playful teasing that makes my legs weaken and my heart race.

And here I thought he would ravage my mouth.

He captures my bottom lip in a kiss, and his tongue slides over it, testing me. I open to his tongue, and he deepens the kiss, filling my senses with nothing but us. He still carries the scent of wood polish and glass cleaner and the masculine spiciness I can't quite name. His arms cinch around my waist and draw me in flat against him. His body is tight and hard against my curves, and the kiss grows more insistent. I need more, and so does he. I can feel it in my blood and in the way his fingers gently press into my sides. He's holding back, trying not to dig in. Seducing me with his lips, but the seduction is already complete. I'm soaking wet, and I need him now.

"Let's go," I rasp, gathering up my things, which he promptly takes from me.

Quint mumbles something about stopping to buy condoms.

"I'm on birth control for acne; let's do this," I tell him. Reckless? Sure. There's nothing safe about what we're about to do.

He answers with one of his signature, "yes, ma'am's," as I aimlessly speed-walk down a side street behind a church, then another road, and another, until I find an out-of-the-way cobblestone alleyway between a closed down restaurant and a roped-off entryway to a park.

At the entrance to the park, a sign in Italian reads, "Closed for repairs." I understand just enough Italian, thank god.

The perfect spot.

Chapter Eight

Quint

I DON'T KNOW who spots the empty park first. I don't know whose idea it is to walk right through the barricade, ignoring the "closed" sign. Ally and I are a hive mind with a single goal.

Hand in hand, with me, loaded down with bags and parcels, we quietly follow a winding brick path along a grove of trees. The pathway bends into the woods, ending at a small bench that looks out into a small clearing filled with bird feeders, baths, and other things I only casually notice.

I drop everything and drag Ally into my lap, hooking her legs around my waist as we resume kissing.

"Quint, I've never done things like this in public before," she says.

I smirk. "All the parts work the same way as they do in private."

She puffs out a small laugh, and I use this moment to

show her exactly what she does to me. After some unbuck-
ling, unzipping, and adjusting, I let Ally watch as I fist my
cock in my hand. Ally's eyes widen, her mouth goes slack
as she takes in the sight of my rigid length.

"Quint. What happened to the guy who couldn't even
look me in the eyes?"

Gritting my teeth, I tell her the truth. "He's been trying
to keep his shit together. I try to avoid thinking about you,
looking at you, and imagining how I could take you.
Seeing you sprawled out on my bed. Bent over. Up against
the wall. I've been telling myself I'm too old for you. I
finally gave in. You've destroyed every last fiber of my
resolve. Look at me. Look what you do to me."

Her eyes flash to mine, then back down as she pushes
my hand away and takes my cock in hers. Her touch sends
me into orbit, her thumb swiping over the sensitive tip.

I rumble out her name as all the blood leaves my brain.

"I don't know if I can take all of this inside me," she
says.

"We can do some warm-up stretches first," I answer.

"Oh my gosh, I love your dirty mouth," she murmurs
against my lips as we share a heated kiss.

I grip her hips and move her on me, grinding her body
up and down against my aching dick. We're so snug and
tight in this magical little alcove, and it feels like our own
kingdom that we have all to ourselves.

I need more of her. I need more than just to get each
other off in a hurry. We don't have much time, but I need
more. More skin, more kissing, more of her.

"Take your top off."

"Yes, Daddy," she says breathily, winking.

I help Ally pull off her top over her head while she
unhooks her bra. I gently fold her top and set it down on
the bench.

When her bra falls away and her breasts are exposed, I feel like I've come home.

I'm hit with an overwhelming need to say more. "Ally. I have to tell you something. I don't mess around with guests. I don't mess around with random women at all. I want you to know that you are safe with me, and I'm not letting you go. I don't know what that will look like, but whatever happens, you're mine. You're my girl."

"Quint," she squeaks, grinding against me. "I'm not supposed to be catching feelings; I'm supposed to be figuring out my life. But when I'm with you, I don't care about anything. I only wanted your hands on me. I thought I would have fun messing with you, but you had to go and buy all those books. All those fucking books. God, you pretend to hate me, and you go and do things, and I feel like I'm falling apart."

Hushing her with a deep kiss, I absorb every word.

We're done talking now. My mouth has other plans, mainly worshiping her tempting breasts. Full and soft and right where they need to be. I nuzzle against them, cupping them and kissing them. The mild teasing of my mouth and the gentle handling draws a sexy whimper out of her.

"Quint, I need…oh god…."

I'll be the first to admit I feel pretty damn wickedly satisfied that she's begging for it. But I'm not done. Sucking one nipple into my mouth, I slowly savor it, drawing out the hard bud with my tongue and teeth. Ally bucks against me as I repeat the same thing with her opposite nipple. She's so soft, smells so delicately floral and spicy, I want to take all day. I could spend hours, days in these woods just tasting every inch, claiming every spot on her body.

Finally, I give in, not in small part, because our phones are blowing up with texts and unanswered phone calls.

We're so fucked. Everyone on the yacht is now wondering when we're coming back.

"Get rid of those pants," I tell Ally. She slides off my lap just long enough to wiggle out of her jeans and panties, unintentionally giving me a delightful show with her bouncing, lovely tits.

She is now totally exposed, should anyone walk up on us.

Lifting her up, I seat Ally on my cock and let her guide me in, slowly stretching. There may be nothing more erotic in this world than her face while she notices her body adjusting to me, taking me a little at a time.

At the same time, I feel her sweetness overwhelm me, surrounding my cock with her heat.

My Ally is so tight…so good, so wet, so tight. I almost cannot breathe. I watch her for any clues of discomfort, but soon I'm seated fully inside her core, her arms hugging my neck and her eyes blazing. It's almost unbelievable but yet so real; I feel Ally under my skin, in my lungs. Everywhere.

We are two wild creatures, fused together and aching for release. She moves, and I move, building joyful but urgent friction that grows with every push and pull and thrust. Every kiss to her lips, shoulders, neck, and breast gets Ally wetter. Our slick connection becomes more frantic, more animalistic with every slap of skin against skin.

I look down at where our two forms connect, and I'm ready to burst. Slowing my thrusts, I explore her with my hands, spreading her folds and finding her warm, tight bundle of nerves. I massage her with my thumb, reveling in how lovely she is when her jaw drops and lets out a hoarse moan.

I thumb her clit, noticing how her beautiful cunt sucks me in and out with greater speed.

My Ally shatters around me with a cry that startles the songbirds, sending them bursting from their perches in the trees around us.

The surprise and delight on her face push me over the edge, and my release takes hold. I come inside her, pumping until there's not a single drop left.

Our phones continue to blow up even as we hold each other through her sweet, trembling aftershocks. I paint her face with kisses, cover her bare flesh with reassuring caresses.

When my shattered brain cells once again form a coherent thought, I have a suggestion.

Ally beats me to it.

"I'm starving," she says as she slides off me and hurriedly shoves on her clothes. "What are you in the mood for?"

"I'm in the mood for dessert between your legs, but I'll settle for actual food until I can get you alone again."

Ally looks at me with mischief in her eyes. "I have to be back to the boat. I'm already late, and you're probably in trouble."

There's too much to say right now. I want to tell her to forget the boat. Come to a hotel with me. I just want to be with her.

"Fuck that. Let's never go back."

I don't know what I'm saying, but I just blurt it out.

"That's cute. Sure, Quint. Let's just run away and start a new life together."

"We should," I say. "Fuck the boat. Fuck your brother. Let's disappear in the city and have some fun."

"Didn't we just do that?"

"We didn't do half the things I want to do with you, Ally."

A wicked smile crosses her lips, and she falls against my

chest, turning her face up for a kiss. Tenderly, I deliver on that kiss with an ache in my heart. "I'm afraid if we keep up this exhibitionism, we'll get charged with a crime."

I open my mouth to tell her that's not what I meant. Sure, I want to keep exploring each other's bodies. But more than that, I want to spend time with her. I want to show her art galleries and libraries and all that interests her.

But we don't get that chance.

Someone is shouting at us in Italian.

"Oh shit," Ally hisses, hurriedly adjusting her clothes. I bolt to my feet and put all my bits back into my drawers. I see someone in a police uniform headed our way down the path.

This is not good.

Ally looks at me and says, "What do we do?"

I grab her hand and say, "Run."

Chapter Nine

Ally

I'VE NEVER RUN SO FAST in my life. I have to if only to keep up with Quint. I call upon my cross-country running skills, which have been a little rusty since high school.

At the dock, I take a flying leap and land in the tender a little too forcefully, and I hear the snap before I feel the pain.

Ignoring it, I help Quint scramble at the knots once he's inside the boat.

It takes a comical number of tries to start the engine. What is it with motorboat engines and not simply starting when you pull the cord? What a terrible design, I think.

Quint speeds us away from the dock just as the policeman on the moped closes in. I wave goodbye, but inside, my heart is racing.

When the tender approaches the stern of *The Carpe Diem*, Elijah, my brother, Juno, and the captain are all assembled there waiting for us.

My brother can see it all over my face. I've been up to something, and I've gotten someone else caught up in my shenanigans. If only he understood. If only he understood what it means to have fun and let loose. Break the rules. He's never broken a single rule, so why would he?

My heart is in my throat. I almost wish we would have taken a gamble with the police instead of this crowd.

"Let me explain," I say this to the captain and not to my brother. I'm more worried about the repercussions for Quint than for me. The captain is ignoring me entirely and starting in on Quint. "You were supposed to have her back on the boat hours ago. What the hell happened?"

The captain is not yelling. He's quietly angry, and the menacing sound in his voice makes me want to jump into the water to hide.

Quint doesn't answer until the boat is tied off to the swim deck. He hops off and reaches for me. I reach out for him, and that's when my brother, who has been quiet up until now, loses it when he sees me limping.

"What happened to you?"

The captain finally notices it, too, the black and blue that is spreading across my skin. "Oh, Jesus." Captain Joe radios for the yacht medic.

Quint gingerly picks me up in his arms, sets me onto the swim deck, and sits down next to me while we wait for the medic.

My brother and the captain, and Elijah are freaking out as I sit there with my leg stretched out on the platform. They all hover, not daring to touch it. Juno shrieks when she sees my injury.

"There are too many people," Captain Joe barks. "Everyone get the hell away from her while we wait for the medic. I don't want to move her."

"I'm not going anywhere, Captain," Quint says.

Captain Joe looks up at us from where he squats, hovering over my ankle. "Son, you're the last person I want to see right now."

I straighten my spine. "He stays, Captain. I need him."

The captain looks at me with a warm, paternal gaze but says nothing. I look from him to Quint, who kneels down beside me.

"I got you," Quint says.

The captain gives Quint a look that communicates lightning, fire, brimstone. Something is going to explode when they talk later, I have a feeling.

I slip my hand into Quint's, and the captain sees.

Captain Joe is seething. "When the medic decides what needs to be done, your ass is on the bridge, Quint. Do you understand me?"

Quint squeezes my hand, and I press back.

He is in so much trouble, and it's all my fault.

That's when a wave of sadness hits me. The dress. The books. The shoes. All the stuff I bought—we left it at the park.

Chapter Ten

Quint

THE MEDIC HAS TAKEN Ally to the infirmary, and Captain has hauled my ass up to the bridge.

I refused to leave her side, but Ally finally persuaded me to go.

Her words to me threw me for a loop. "Don't jeopardize your job for me. You did nothing wrong. It was my fault. I was messing with you. I'll make sure the captain knows I manipulated the entire situation and that I insisted on running off. Go."

I search her eyes for something more, but she looks away.

Heartbroken and confused, I follow the captain up to the bridge.

The captain's eyes are going to pop out of his face.

"No disrespect, Captain," I say, which is always the preamble to much disrespect. "But I seem to recall that you performed an actual wedding between a deckhand

and the daughter of a primary guest before I joined this crew?"

The captain narrows his ice-blue eyes at me. "That was different."

"How?"

"Because I'm your captain, that's the fuck why!"

I know better than to push. I understand rank and protocol, maybe better than anyone on this vessel other than the captain. "You did it because you had something to prove to the monarchy of Austero. You said so yourself. My motives for giving Ally a little bit of freedom also had a point. Her brother is a controlling jerk who refuses to see her as anything but a delinquent kid."

Okay, I know I'm stretching the truth a bit. I didn't find out about her history until our moment in the dressing room, and by that time, I was mainly thinking with my dick.

The captain scoffs. "Tell me why I shouldn't fire your ass right now."

"I don't know why you shouldn't. I crossed the line. I did it. But so did Abel. So did Vanessa. So that tells me you can throw your dick around all you want, but inside you're a hopeless romantic. Well, guess what: so am I."

By the look on the captain's face, I can't tell if he will fire me or deck me.

"The problem is, I can't be sure you won't keep your dick in your pants for the remainder of the charter," Captain Joe says. "It looks like preferential treatment for you, no matter how I slice it."

I think about what Ally said and try to sort out what was sincere and what was only meant to protect me. "You saw what I saw. She doesn't actually want me. She was messing with me because she was bored, and I got caught up in her little web." It pains me to say these outright lies. I don't even want to save my own ass, but I also have the rest of the crew's tips to think about. If I take all the blame, her brother will take it out of our gratuities.

If this is how she wants to play it, fine. If the captain believes this was a case of a wicked temptress playing with me, the consequences for the crew might be more minor. The captain will have a talk with the brother and smooth things over. I don't know how, but the captain can work magic.

"I need you to put an end to this. This can't happen again," he warns.

Elijah nods. "You're a good deckhand, but I won't protest that much if the captain wants to fire you. I need you focused on your job."

My job. My job was to keep her out of trouble, and I did the opposite. I got her injured. If I hadn't revealed my feelings, we never would have gone to that park, and if we hadn't been running from the cops, her ankle would still be intact.

It takes everything in me not to explode just thinking about her being in the infirmary without me by her side. I have to work hard to keep a lid on my temper and my mouth.

"Just one more thing, Captain. She dropped some of her things. Let me run back to shore and see if I can find her purchases."

Elijah and the captain look at each other, and finally, the captain agrees. It will mean perhaps several more hours away from the woman I love, but it needs to be done. Do I love her? Yes, without question. I'm drawn to her like no one else before. The thought of living out my life without her is unfathomable.

But I never make it back to the tender. On the way to the swim deck, a hand grabs my shoulder and spins me around. Typically, the instigator will find themselves pinned against the wall with my hand around their throat when this happens.

On instinct, I do exactly that.

And that's when I see that it's Denny, Ally's brother.

He's scrabbling at my grip, his eyes wide in surprise.

I immediately let him go. "Sorry, man. I didn't know it was you."

"I need to talk to you," he says, rubbing his throat, his chest heaving. I square my shoulders and get ready to listen.

"Alright, let's go somewhere and talk," I say.

"No, this won't take long. All I have to say to you is stay away from my sister."

What a sad man, and so far in over his head. I've already been warned by the captain and my supervisor. I have no reason to push back at him. What's between Ally and me is worth waiting for, and I'll wait until the second they step off the dock tomorrow. The moment Ally is no longer officially a guest, she's no longer off-limits.

All this is true, but the caged beast inside me wants desperately to push back. Ah, fuck it.

"I will not," I say, as the mental image forms of all our crew's tip circling the drain.

"Excuse me?"

"Excuse you," I say. "She's an adult, and she does what she wants. She didn't lure me in with her wicked ways. Fuck that. I wanted her, so I went after her. And I'll do it again. Because she's mine. Ally is my girl. My woman. I love her, and you can do nothing about it."

"You are so fucking fired," Denny seethes.

I laugh. "Don't bother, dude. I've already turned in my resignation." Yes, this is a lie, but he doesn't get to have a real man-to-man when all he wants to do is throw his dick around. I have no respect or patience for a guest who makes a stew cry over a bad margarita. "I know it feels good to threaten to have people fired and shit, so it must suck to have that power taken away."

Denny puts up two meaty fists. "Then there's only one way to handle this."

"There's no way I'm fighting you, Denny."

I laugh and wave him off and begin to turn away, and that's when everything around me explodes into stars. The impact of Denny's fist to my temple temporarily blinds me, and I stumble backward into someone. When I hit the floor, I'm accompanied by breaking glass and the smell of pale ale. When my eyesight returns half a second later, I'm looking up at a bewildered Juno, who has dropped a beer tray.

"Don't move!" she shouts.

But I don't listen. Why start now?

I heave myself to my feet, ignoring the wooziness in my head, and lunge at Denny. We crash to the floor amid shrieks from the guests, Juno, and other crew members. I don't give a fuck. I nail the man with a crack to the jaw. He roars, then rolls me over, pins me to the floor, and clumsily tries to get me into a headlock. I twist, elbow him in his soft belly, and he groans. I scramble away from him just as Elijah literally picks me up and carries me off in a bear hug from behind. Andre and the first officer are holding Denny back, and I laugh all the way to the infirmary.

I am so fucked.

Chapter Eleven

Quint

I'M FIRED for sure this time.

First, I dismiss the medic, despite his protestations. I can remove glass shards from my own feet.

But first, I go to her. My Ally gapes at me in surprise that turns to concern, then horror, when she sees me wincing with every bloody step.

"Quint, what happened?"

I locate a tweezer, rubbing alcohol, and a bowl, and get to work on my feet.

"Your brother happened." Tiny shards of glass plink into the metal bowl one by one.

"Oh my god. I'm going to kill him."

"I won't stop you. How's the ankle?"

Ally shrugs. "Medic says it's twisted really bad. No breaks, but I'll need to stay off it. How did you get glass in your feet, though? Seriously!"

I laugh. "You don't want to know. Look away, sweetheart, if the sight of blood makes you ill."

She snorts. "I'm fine with a little blood. Spill it."

I tell her the whole story of the fight between her brother and me, and she just looks at me like I've lost my mind.

"You can't go around punching people," she says.

More drops of glass into metal fill the silence between us.

"I know," I say, concentrating on a particularly deep cut in the ball of my foot.

"Especially not my brother. He's not built for fighting."

I blow out a noisy breath. "He got in a few good licks, trust me."

"Yeah, well, you shouldn't have lunged at him. I can't have you losing your job over me."

"I'm fired anyway for what I said, whether or not I decked him."

Ally looks at me hard. "What did you say to him?"

"I told him that you're my girl, and he couldn't keep me away from you. I told him the truth that you didn't do anything to provoke me. That's it. I'm crazy about you, Ally. I was from the beginning. As soon as I saw you, I knew I wasn't going to be able to think about anyone else. I acted the way I did at first because I was fighting myself. I was fighting everything in me that was drawn to you. I was trying to keep my distance. I don't care about my tips, but I didn't want to jeopardize anything for the crew. But after the day we had together, after the time I got to spend with you, I know I want every day to be with you. I can't imagine going through life without you. I want to give it a shot."

By the time I'm finished, Ally's face is pained. "The boat docks tomorrow, and we head back home."

"And? Where do you want to go?"

She gives me a wary smile. "I don't know. I don't want to leave you, either. I'm done giving you the slip. Forever."

A moment passes between us, both of us not sure what will happen next.

Gingerly, I crouch over her cot, careful not to touch her propped-up leg, and kiss her. The joining of our mouths is all too short, but it's full of promise and seals in my mind everything we just said to each other.

"Sweetheart, do you need anything?"

"I'm still kind of hungry. We never did get to have our lunch together."

Smoothing her hair back away from her face, I radio Juno and ask her to have Maksim prepare something for my Ally.

After wrapping up my feet, I test out how it feels to stand on them. It's not great, but all the glass particles are gone.

I lean over and press a kiss to Ally's forehead. "I'll be right back."

When I return with a bowl of soup and a seafood salad for Ally, the room looks like an ambush intervention. I'm trapped in a room with a severe-looking captain and my supervisor twice in one hour. Joining us is her brother.

Ally sits up straight, and I sit next to her, lifting a spoonful of soup to her mouth, ignoring everyone else in the room and ignoring the throbbing in my feet.

"Quint, we've been talking," Elijah says.

"That explains why I wasn't fired on my way to the galley and back."

"I do know how to eat soup," Ally tells me, but I continue to fuss until she lets me feed her. She blushes and rolls her eyes, but she lets me. Good.

I keep my eyes on her even while my bosses are

explaining things to me. I already know I'm up shit's creek Without a paddle. I don't care what more there is to say.

The captain clears his throat. "The thing is, Ally has been looking for a job. She's expressed an interest in working on this boat, and we could always use an extra set of hands. As much as I would love to heave your ass into the drink right now, I think the smarter thing to do would be to make the whole thing right."

Wait, what am I hearing?

I turn around and face the captain. "What's happening?"

"We talked it over, and her brother agrees. If she wants to stay and work on the boat, let her try this out for the remainder of the charter season, I'm good with that. I'm willing to give her a chance if she's willing to work."

I turn back to face Ally, bewildered. She nods enthusiastically. "I'm willing to work. I'm willing to learn anything. If it means you won't fire Quint, I'll try it."

I set down the soup and scrub my hands over my face. "Wait just a minute," I say. "Captain, you aren't letting me go?"

He sits back and exhales heavily. "Looks like I won't have to. As long as the two of you are actually going to work and not make out With each other while you should be working. Can you handle that?"

Ally and I answer simultaneously.

"Yes, Captain," I say.

"No guarantees," Ally says.

Everyone turns to her. "I'm kidding! Wow, I can see everyone has so much faith in me already."

Just then, Juno enters the infirmary, looking a little wary.

"Hi, honey, can I get you anything?" Juno obviously

thinks she was called here for service. "Meet your newest floater," Captain Joe says.

Ally waves.

"Keep an eye on her," Ally's brother says. "She's a slippery one."

I have to fight the urge to lunge at him a second time.

Juno nods and looks Ally over. "How long until you can put weight on it?"

"Probably just a few hours."

"Great. Can you mix a margarita?"

"Of course."

Denny blurts, "How? You're only 19!"

Juno ignores Doug's outburst. "Nineteen, 29, I don't care. This is the Med, not the U.S. As long as you know how to make coffee and mix drinks, I'll put you to work. Welcome aboard."

ALLY MAY scoff at the stack of pillows onto which I prop her ankle in her bed, but I insist.

"Once again, I am fine, Quint. I promise."

I can't help but fuss over her. She's way too precious to me. "You're going to keep it elevated until I'm sure it's totally healed."

Wiggling her toes and pointing at the spot where a bruise used to be, she exclaims, "Look! Not even a bruise. Nor a twinge! I am injury-free, I promise."

Running my hand down the soft skin of her elevated calf, I reply, "We'll have the medic check you over again tomorrow."

She looks at me like I'm being unreasonable on another level. "Please don't bother the medic anymore.

You had him check me over like three different times today. He does have to tend to other things on this boat."

Her skin feels hot to the touch, so I test the temperature on her forehead.

"What are you doing?"

"You feel feverish," I say.

A slow smile spreads across her face. "Oh. I am feverish."

Panic rises in my throat. "You are? When did this start? I'm waking up the medic right now."

I move to get up and fetch my radio. "Don't you dare," she growls, gripping the front of my shirt and yanking me down on top of her.

"Baby," I say. "You might be sick."

"I'm not sick. I'm feverish and hot because I require attention."

I stare at her and wonder if she's so ill that she's speaking gibberish. "Then you should let me go call the medic. I'm worried about you, baby."

She makes sure I understand what she means by hooking her non-injured leg around my thigh and pulling me closer.

"Not. That. Kind of attention." Ally murmurs these words close to me, then punctuates it with a gentle nip one of the tensed cords along my neck.

"Oh," I sigh in relief mixed with a quickly growing hunger. "But…your ankle."

With her fist gripping my shirt, she pushes me away slightly to meet my eyes. "The use of my ankle is not necessary for carrying out these attention-seeking activities."

I want to. Damn, do I want to do whatever she wants at any time, anywhere. I can't resist her touch, her closeness, her scent. All of her. I want all of her all the time. But when she's laid up with a bum ankle? Would it be right? Wouldn't that make me a bad guy taking advantage of someone who can't run away?

"Baby," I say, trying to pull away, but she tugs me back. I don't resist. I simply cannot. "You're making it hard to keep Nurse Quint and Boyfriend Quint separate."

The arch in her eyebrow further erodes my ability to resist the stroking of her thigh up and down my back and the friction at her core every time one of us moves a single inch. "You can be my nurse boyfriend."

I smile and angle my face to dot small kisses along her neck. A neck nuzzle for a neck nuzzle. "That sounds like something that could get my medical license removed," I say, playing along with her little game.

"Ohh. I love it when you break the rules with me," she purrs.

Her lips swipe across mine, her breath tickling the stubble on my chin.

The question I have is a dangerous one. Once I ask it, the answer will determine my next move, and I already know that move will make me the guy who fucked his girlfriend while she was injured. But…is that a bad thing? I don't know. "What does a nurse boyfriend do?"

She hums, and our bodies are so close that the noise creates a vibration between us.

Her pelvis rocks forward into mine. "Whatever he wants. As long as he does it really, really slowly."

The noise from my throat is almost unhinged as I let go of my inner restraint.

First, I shove up the hem of her shirt and ravenously, wetly, kiss my way down her sweet belly.

Her pajama bottoms come off with little effort. "Nurse

Quint is pleased with your lack of underwear," I murmur against the bare skin below her navel.

"Oh my god, don't talk to me down there," she breathes.

I stop and look up, noticing her flushed. "You okay?"

She nods and bites her lip. "Uh-huh. It just…makes me extra wet when you do that."

I should stop. I should do precisely as she says. But now I'm intrigued. Feathering my lips over her skin, just above the juncture of her thighs, I say more. "Like this? Is this what I'm not supposed to do?"

Ally hisses. "Quint, oh my god."

My lips press small, sultry kisses all over her lower abdomen, slowly, sweetly, until Ally writhes and bucks under me. "Easy, sweetheart. Let me test out that claim."

Keeping her injured leg still, I spread the other one wide. The source of her scent envelops me with her spicy floral essence. She gasps when my thumbs spread open her folds, and I begin to lick her there. Holy hell, she was not exaggerating.

"Baby, finding you so wet just got me unbelievably hard."

Ally's body stiffens at the contact of my mouth, my tongue, my breath, and then she melts. I ease my tongue through her sweetness, losing myself in her. The more I drink from her, the more she gives me. The more she gives, the more I take, and I become more intoxicated.

"Quint, holy shit…oh my god."

Her taut bundle of nerves is warm on my tongue, and I gently cover it with my mouth and suck. Ally fists my hair as her body bucks against my face.

She comes apart with a shudder. Watching her back arch off the bed, listening to her moans—all of it drives me closer to spilling my seed all over myself.

But that can wait. It will have to wait. As bad as I want to be buried inside my woman, my first duty is to make sure she's fully healed. Because she's in for a fucking ride.

Chapter Twelve

Ally

Two nights later, I say goodbye to my luxury cabin and move my things into Quint's bunk.

My brother and I said goodbye on basically good terms. Not great, not strictly at odds anymore. I'd call it reluctant acceptance. And I got control of my accounts. As for him and Quint? They'll work it out. As long as they can avoid a fistfight the next time they see each other.

This is also the day I begin taking my meals below deck.

"These bunks are like musical chairs. With the way people pair off, you never know who will want to move in together from one night to the next," Star informs me as we eat our evening meal in the crew mess when I apologize for intruding.

Chef Maksim has prepared a mountain of food. While it's more casual than the fancy dinners above deck, I prefer it. Some of the crew plans a night on the town, and tomorrow we prep the boat for the next charter. We have a day off the day after that, and I'm looking forward to another fun adventure with Quint. Maybe we can go back to that bookstore, and I can find one of the books that I lost. I hate having to buy another copy after Quint was so sweet to pick them up for me, but it is what it is.

I examine my new coworkers while I eat, wondering if we'll all get along. Especially since Quint isn't here. Earlier, he said he had some errands to run, but he would be back tonight after I finish helping clean the cabins.

Later that evening, after completing my shift, I shower in our tiny head that adjoins Quint's room, then fall asleep listening to music. At the same time, I wait for Quint to come back. I have to focus on something because I'm starting to get worried. I thought he said he needed to pick some things up for the next charter. I'd thought that was weird because usually, the chief stew and the chef make provisioning trips.

I don't know how long I've been asleep, but I wake up to the sensation of heat from someone's body as they slide in next to me on the bottom bunk.

Quint's legs tangle with mine. He's warm and smells like the outdoors at the height of summer.

I open my eyes, but I can see very little in this dark bunk. He presses a kiss to my forehead, and I mumble, "Is it morning?"

"No, baby," he whispers. "Go back to sleep."

"Where were you?"

"I had to take care of some stuff," he says.

"You weren't getting into fights, were you?"

He quietly hums as I drag my thigh upward. I instantly grow wet as he welcomes that thigh, running a hand over my rump and squeezing.

"Yep. I laid waste to all our enemies," he teases me and kisses my lips. I know he's trying to change the subject.

"Quint. I was worried you got caught by the police."

"For what?" His roaming hands drag down my ass, his fingers swiping sneakily over my split. The cluster of nerves there explodes in pleasure at the contact, and I suck in a breath.

"Naughty boy. Remember when we were being chased through the streets?"

Quint hums against my mouth, his teeth playing with my bottom lip. "Oh, that. Well, as a matter of fact, I did run into that cop. It was funny."

I nearly hit my head, sitting up in shock. "What? Oh no. What did you do?"

He makes a noise of feigning offense. "Nothing! We worked out a deal. Now get back down here and give me that ass."

This makes me laugh and excites me at the same time. My soft laughter into his mouth turns into moans as he swipes his hands all over my backside, teasing my split, igniting interesting sensations in that tight inner spot.

In ten seconds, I went from asleep to turned on so thoroughly that I'll never sleep if we don't demolish each other right now.

"What kind of a deal?"

Quint hums and answers me with a dark chuckle. The next moment, our clothes are shoved off and lie in a crumpled heap somewhere in the corner of the bunk.

Being fully naked with him in the darkness hits different from being naked with him outside in the daytime. I can't see what's coming, and it's delicious anticipation.

That anticipation is rewarded when he attacks me with his mouth…everywhere. I forget my questions about where he was and who he talked to. Quint tastes my essence, drawing out a fast climax from me and sharing my taste in a deep, tonguing kiss. I'm barely recovered from the trembling when he notches his hard length into me and thrusts home.

"Oh my god." I need to come up with some original dirty talk, but I'm just so full of him. Quint slides out slowly and pumps. Then again, and again. Every ridge of him, every movement, makes my body sing. I'm overwhelmed by his rough touch, followed by gentle touches, his girth, his mouth, his everything. I'm simply lost in pleasure. I'm lost in my man. My Quint.

I didn't think my need could explode and rebuild quickly, but his fingers are wicked and will not stop exploring my rump, my clit. He ravishes my breasts with his mouth. I can do nothing but writhe and buck, moan and pull his hair. We fit so tight together; he's so big inside me, it should hurt, but my sex craves more of him. More pumping, more deep thrusting.

Suddenly, he stills. Gasping, my hands let go of his hair and scramble around the sheets for purchase. My thighs clamp down, demanding him to keep going. But he's utterly still. A half grunt, a half whimper escapes me. "Please," I beg.

Rough fingers brush against my sweat-soaked forehead. His breath against my collarbone, my neck, is not helping me calm down if that's what he intends.

"Shhh. Just hold on. I need to tell you something."

I urge him on with a breathless sort-of whine. "Tell me. Quickly."

He presses a kiss to my forehead. "I love you, Ally. You're mine, and I love you."

Below the waist, my body is shrieking inwardly in frustration. The rest of me warms at his words. I wrap my arms around him, clinging to him, and laugh. "Remember when I thought you hated my guts? Less than a week ago?"

He chuckles softly and kisses me with a tenderness that squeezes out all further comments from me. "I never did. I loved your guts from day one."

Snaking my fingers through his hair, I tell him the truth. "And I love you and your guts."

"Forever," he says. And I notice it is a statement, not a question.

"Forever," I repeat after him.

Quint flips me onto my stomach without another warning and bends me at the waist. I gasp and cry out in surprise and excitement. He slaps into my cunt from behind, back to where he belongs. I take all of it, all of him, over and over, in a relentless erotic rhythm. The movement hits me in that inner spot, driving me headlong into a shattering release.

Strangled curses rip from our throats as he spills his seed into me, and we are spent. Gasping for breath, he rolls me on top of his chest.

My body is still thrumming. My heart still pounding. But my mind and my soul calm as we talk. We talk about important things, unimportant things. Silly things and dark things.

We make plans for the future and reveal secrets, and we join together again. This time, we are slow and sweet with each other. I never understood the phrase "making love" until now. We are simply two fools who can't escape each other. And I never want to give him the slip again.

"I got your stuff back, by the way," he says casually, sleepily.

"What?" I barely remember what we were talking about, then it hits me.

"My books?"

"Yep. And the shoes. And the sunglasses and other shit. And I made another side trip to repurchase the dress."

Once again, I sit up and almost hit my head on the top bunk, but Quint is quick to prevent that. He drags me back down to him, and I let him.

"How?"

"Let's just say I've gotten in several fights in several countries in my Navy and yachting career. Let's also say that I have learned how to bribe cops in several different languages. He might've kept the stuff, but he let it go."

I know there's no point telling Quint he's done too much for me. I know he'll never listen when I tell him not to make a fuss.

"You didn't have to get the dress. I missed the formal dinner with the captain because of my ankle," I say.

"But you'll need it for our wedding," he says.

My insides light up. Wedding dress?

I don't know whether to squeal at this quasi-proposal, kiss him for knowing how much I love the dress, or deck him for assuming that we're getting married.

I know that's the kind of feeling he will provoke in me for the rest of our lives.

And I'm good with that.

Epilogue

Ten years later

QUINT

ALLY KNOWS what it does to me when she wears those shoes.

At the moment, I've got my hands full of pieces of an elementary school science project. So I can't really do anything about the stirring below my navel.

Those six-inch stilettos have featured heavily in our bed the first nine years of marriage.

Up until Valentine's Day last year.

That's when the biopsy results came back with unthinkable news.

My chest tightens as I watch my wife strap on those heels for the first time in a year, a scarf still covering her head. Her hair is growing back quickly now that she's finished her treatments and all her follow up tests have shown excellent results.

I watch Ally fuss over our three kids, loading them into the car, wondering what's gotten into her.

After buckling the kids into the back seats and shutting the door, she strolls around to the other side, ensuring my eyes are trained on her enticing hip sway.

She's got me thinking of things, wicked things, while we're supposed to be in "upstanding PTA parents" mode.

Thinking of all those things while I'm loading the entire solar system into the car's trunk is going to give me balls even more blue than Neptune.

I back my wife into the passenger side door. "And where do you think you're going in those shoes?" I ask, pressing my lips against her neck.

"To the science fair! Where do you think I'm going?"

I eyeball my wife as I buckle her in. She tries to swat me away, but I insist. We do this every time we drive anywhere together.

"What are you up to?" I ask Ally.

She blinks up at me, much like she did that day on the yacht when she'd asked me to apply her sunscreen. "Nothing? Why would I be up to something? Today is about Adam, remember?"

After another five years spent in yachting, both Ally and I worked our way up the ranks. Since Adam and the other little ones came along, we've settled down in Chicago near my brother, where Ally runs a small used bookstore, and I work as a firefighter. Since we both miss the water, we make a point to take trips to the beach every summer as often as we can.

I'm still questioning my wife's shoe choice while sitting through the science presentations in the elementary school gym. We sit in the front row, perched on the edge of our seats when Adam takes the stage. When he finishes his speech and flips the switch, the little Lego device he assembled — all on his own — makes the planets and moons rotate around the sun. It had taken him seventeen tries at home to get it to work, so Ally and I leap up and cheer raucously as everyone stares.

We are officially "those" parents.

After the fair, the teacher pulls me aside to talk to me about entering Adam's project into a state competition.

I don't see Ally anywhere, but my brother, Jake, is keeping all three kids occupied with a basketball game.

Then, my eyes finally land on my wife. Ally is nibbling on a cookie, sitting on a folding chair with her legs crossed, bouncing one leg. As the teacher is talking, I can't help but feel distracted as another pair of eyes lands on my wife's feet.

Oh, hell no.

The PTA president is sidling up to my wife, his eyes nearly popping out of his skull. The man looks like he might be about to drool all over my woman.

I stand back and low-key watch what happens next. He's standing too close to her, pretending to politely wait his turn to get her attention. Ally, for her part, is talking to a friend and completely ignoring Jason.

I force myself to turn my attention back to Adam's teacher because I know I'm being rude. The two of us finish our chat, and I'm left alone to seethe in my jealousy from this dark corner of the gym.

I've seen how that guy stares at my wife at PTA meetings. In the past, I'd chalked it up to him being interested in her ideas for how to raise money for the school.

But it's not just that guy. I look around the room, and I can count five, six, seven dudes staring at my wife's legs.

That's when I snap.

I march past my brother, and without even looking at him, I ask, "Can you…?"

"I'll take the kids out for ice cream," he assures me, clearly noticing what's going on.

It only takes five strides to get next to my wife, but it may as well be fifteen thousand; that's how it feels whenever I need to get her away from the public eye.

Her eyes widen as I approach. Without glancing at her friend, I thread my fingers through Ally's and pull her away.

Her friend has seen this behavior from me before, laughs, and says goodbye.

"Quint, what are you doing? I was in the middle of a conversation!" Ally hisses.

I say nothing until we're in the parking lot, and I've got her pinned under me in the back of the suburban.

Gripping one ankle in my hand, I press a kiss along the arch of her foot, then slowly drag my mouth upward until I've painted every inch of tender skin inside her calf. Then, I shove her legs apart and hike up her skirt.

Brushing my lips against her thigh, I finally speak. "You think I don't know what you're doing? Are you trying to make me jealous? Bad girl."

Ally sucks in a breath as I press my lips against the damp crotch of her panties.

"I wasn't!"

"You play your little games, and I have to take you to the car to punish you."

She protests again, breathlessly, but I hook my thumb in the panties and tug them to the side. I carry out her repercussions by pushing my tongue inside her heat, tasting her wetness.

"If you weren't trying to make me jealous, why are you so wet, baby girl?"

Ally moans and grinds against my face, begging for more contact.

"Why?" I seethe.

On a whimper, she blurts, "I just wanted to wear the shoes for you…to get you excited for later. I didn't intend anything else by it. I don't give a fuck about attention from anyone else. Oh, shit, Quint!"

I've shoved her undies down to her calves, and I'm thoroughly gorging myself on her sweetness. My wife's essence gushes into my mouth; every inch of her is like honey straight from a goddess.

I release a chuckle as her fingers tangle in my hair.

I do my worst, covering her with kisses, nibbling, and suckling until Ally bucks against me and her thighs tremble. Covering her clit with my mouth, I nudge her to completion. She falls apart, squeaking out my name.

She is so loud and animated when she comes, even after all this time.

She doesn't need to wear those heels, and she doesn't need to play games.

I will take her anywhere and everywhere. Shoes or no shoes. Dressed or not.

We can do this two, three, or four times a day and not get tired. Because we trust each other. Because we are insatiable with one another. I can't get enough of her body, mind, and soul.

After three kids and a long journey through illness, we've come out on the other side with sweet rewards.

The best part of this is the end when I get to wrap her up in my arms and feel her heartbeat against mine.

"I've got you, sweetheart," I say, sharing a soft kiss to her lips.

Ally returns the sentiment, stroking my face. "I think about the time we spent in our bed and you held me throughout my treatments. Even In my hospital bed. You always made sure our hearts connected. Thank you for that."

"You missed out on so much while you were sick; I felt like that was the least I could do."

Ally smiles at me, and I'm reminded of our time together in the tight bunk aboard The Carpe Diem. Our legs tangle together in just the same way.

"You were, and are, beyond the best," she replies.

I hum as I place a kiss to her temple, contemplating whether to give her her present early.

"Ah, what the hell," I say. Shifting her weight closer to me, I grab for the bag at the back of the small space, reach inside and hand her the small package.

She sits up and runs her hands over it. "Quint, what is this? What did you do?"

I click on the flashlight on my phone and hover it over the package so she can see what's she's doing. "Open it."

When she finds the personalized inscription on the title page, her hand goes to her mouth.

I'd written a letter to Ally's favorite author, telling her about her journey and how we'd met. The author had replied with a personalized copy for Ally. I hadn't even read what she wrote.

All I can see is Ally's hands covering her mouth.

She drops the book, and I catch it.

"Is it good?" I ask.

Ally only nods her head.

I read the inscription, and it's perfect.

"Wishing you all the best, through all the awesome, challenging, and life-changing moments yet to come. Life will give and take, but nothing can take away your story."

. . .

THE END

Thank you for reading Decked! If you enjoyed this book, please consider leaving a review. Don't forget to check out the other stories in the Naughty Yachties series, and all of my other books listed on my website at authorabbyknox.com!

About the Author

Abby Knox writes feel-good, high-heat romance that she herself would want to read. Readers have described her stories as quirky, sexy, adorable, and hilarious. All of that adds up to Abby's overall goal in life: to be kind and to have fun!

Abby's favorite tropes include: Forced proximity, opposites attract, grumpy/sunshine, age gap, boss/employee, fated mates/insta-love, and more. Abby is heavily influenced by Buffy the Vampire Slayer, Gilmore Girls, and LOST. But don't worry, she won't ever make you suffer like Luke & Lorelai.

If any or all of that connects with you, then you came to the right place.